About the A

With over a decade of experience in television, video and audio production, Kimberley grew up in rural North Devon before venturing to London to pursue her career in media. In 2018 she won the media category at the Women of the Future Awards.

Other than her marriage and the birth of her daughter Florence, one of Kimberley's proudest achievements to date has been her work on the Telegraph's 'Mad World' podcast, working closely with journalist Bryony Gordon to reflect to the wider audience why sometimes in life it's perfectly normal to feel weird.

This sentiment, alongside her own experiences of living in both the city and countryside, is the inspiration behind Townie Spider.

Townie Spider

Kimberley Rowell

Townie Spider

Olympia Publishers
London

www.olympiapublishers.com
OLYMPIA PAPERBACK EDITION

A CIP catalogue record for this title is
available from the British Library.

ISBN: 978-1-78830-334-7

First Published in 2019

Olympia Publishers
60 Cannon Street
London
EC4N 6NP

Printed in Great Britain

Dedication

For Florence

Acknowledgements

Huge thanks to Olympia Publishers for setting me off on this journey.

To Lauren, Alan and Laura for believing in me.

To my mum Denise, dad Nigel, husband Bernie and daughter Florence.
Without you, there is no me.

Townie Spider had a bit of a problem
Of which he was not very fond.
He'd fallen asleep in London Town
And woken in the back of beyond.

The last thing that he could recollect
Being so conveniently small.
Was curling up inside a cavernous space
And bidding, "good night one and all."

Now the one thing that Townie was not to know
Was the cavernous space was a mirror
Attached to a humanoid's pride and joy,
An Audi Q6 called Camilla.

The humanoid had chosen that very night
To venture down south to the country.
Choosing the main roads and highways
Meant the journey was smooth and not bumpy

For Townie curled up in the cavernous hole
Really was none the wiser.
Until the next morning when venturing outside
And being met by a sheepdog called Kaiser

"Excuse me good fellow," said Townie
"Could you tell me please where we are?"
"Well this is Giggleton Farm," he replied
"And you're in the master's son's car."

Townie turned a shade of pale
And pulled all eight legs to his tummy.
He was further from home than he'd ever been
And could do with a hug from his mummy.

Seeing his new friend look frightened
Wanting to be helpful and kind.
Old Kaiser took matters to his own paws
Certain his master wouldn't mind.

“Hop on my ears,” the sheepdog said.
“Let’s find you some friendly faces.
Although on first glimpse the farmyard’s immense
It’s really the nicest of places.”

Tentatively unfurling his legs one by one
Townie took the dog on his word.
But underestimating the distance between dog and car
Landed on a rather warm turd

Lowering his snout to the spider's level
Doing his best not to chuckle.
Kaiser whisked poor Townie away
Nestled in the flea collar's buckle.

As Kaiser bounded off to the cowshed
Townie clung to the dog for dear life.
Lamenting how he'd gone from civilised safety
Ending up in such trouble and strife.

They came to a stop by some railings
Coming face-to-face with Gertrude a Friesian.
Who continued munching her straw and hay
Food interruption needed good reason.

"I'm looking for Den and Nuggin,
Have you seen them today?" Kaiser posed.
"They're sunning themselves by the pond," Gertrude said
With a friendly lick of the nose.

Locating the farmyard fox and mole
Dozing beneath a sycamore tree.
The commotion of a lolloping sheepdog
Soon broke their reverie.

"Guys, I'd like to introduce you to Townie
He's lost and far from home,
Let's give him a countryside welcome
And show him you're never alone."

Townie opened four of his eyes
Feeling safe with just half.
Being met with the smiles of a fox, mole and dog
He couldn't help but laugh.

The inquisitive trio made an unusual bunch
"Well hi there, newbie," said Den.
"Nuggin and I will show you around the place,
We'll soon be the best of friends."

And that's how it came to pass you see
This unlikely band of comrades.
The very start of their story
And all challenges they faced on the way.